Moses Goes
to a Concert

ISAAC MILLMAN

Frances Foster Books • Farrar, Straus and Giroux • New York

In tender memory of
Rivelé and Moische Sztrymfman
Your loving son

Copyright © 1998 by Isaac Millman
All rights reserved
Distributed in Canada by Douglas & McIntyre Ltd.
Printed and bound in the United States of America by Berryville Graphics
Designed by Filomena Tuosto
First edition, 1998
Fourth printing, 1999

Library of Congress Cataloging-in-Publication Data
Millman, Isaac.
   Moses goes to a concert / Isaac Millman. — 1st ed.
      p.   cm.
   "Frances Foster books."
   Summary: Moses and his schoolmates, all deaf, attend a concert where
the orchestra's percussionist is also deaf. Includes illustrations in sign
language and a page showing the manual alphabet.
   [1. Deaf—Fiction. 2. Physically handicapped—Fiction. 3. Percussion
instruments—Fiction. 4. Musicians—Fiction. 5. Sign language.] I. Title.
PZ7.M63954Mo   1998
[E]—dc21   97-2930

AUTHOR'S NOTE

Most people in the deaf community communicate with one another in American Sign Language, which is often called by its initials, ASL. ASL is a visual sign language which is composed of precise handshapes, movements, and facial expressions that are used to form words. I am indebted to Dorothy Cohler and Joel Goldfarb, Deaf teachers at New York City's J.H.S. 47 School for the Deaf, for the many hours they spent helping me get the sign-language diagrams in this book right. If you follow carefully the position of the hands and fingers and the direction of the arrows shown in the diagrams, you can begin to learn a few words in American Sign Language. You can also learn the hand alphabet, which is pictured on the last page of this book.

HOW TO READ THE ARROWS AND SYMBOLS

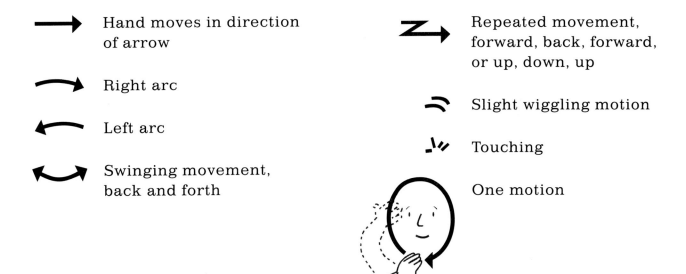

Moses plays on his new drum.
He can't hear the sounds he is making because he is deaf, but he feels the vibration of the drum through his hands. He has taken off his shoes so he can feel it through his feet, too.

| I | PLAY | THE DRUM |

Today, Moses is going on a field trip. His teacher, Mr. Samuels, is taking him and his classmates, who are all deaf, to a young people's concert.

As the children climb onto the bus, they wonder what is inside Mr. Samuels's black bag.

"A big surprise," signs Mr. Samuels.

THE TEACHER   HAS   A BIG SURPRISE

On the bus, Moses signs to his friend. "John! My parents gave me a new drum!"
John signs back. "I got one, too!"

MY   FRIEND

Children from all over the city are coming to the concert. Moses and his friend John wait for their class to get off the bus so they can go inside together.

Mr. Samuels leads them to their seats in the first row. Across the stage, in front of the orchestra, are all the percussion instruments. "Children, the percussionist is a friend of mine," signs Mr. Samuels. "What's a percussionist?" Anna signs back.
"A musician who plays an instrument such as a drum, cymbals, even a piano," replies Mr. Samuels.

A young woman walks onto the stage. Everyone stands up to applaud. Some of Moses's classmates wave instead of clapping. The percussionist smiles and bows to the audience.

WE   WAVE   AND   APPLAUD

"She has no shoes!" Moses signs in surprise.

The teacher smiles and signs, "She is deaf, too. She follows the orchestra by feeling the vibrations of the music through her stocking feet."

Then Mr. Samuels takes eleven balloons out of his black bag and hands one to each of his students.

"Oh! What beautiful balloons!" Anna signs.

"Hold them on your laps," signs Mr. Samuels. "They'll help you feel the music."

ELEVEN BEAUTIFUL BALLOONS

The conductor turns to face the orchestra and raises his baton.
The percussionist strikes the huge gong and the concert begins.

The percussionist watches the conductor and moves from one instrument to the next, striking each to make a sound. Moses and his classmates hold their balloons in their laps. They can feel the music as their balloons pick up the vibrations.

I   FEEL   VIBRATIONS

When the concert is over, Mr. Samuels has another surprise. He takes the children onstage to meet his friend, Ms. Marjorie Elwyn. "She will tell you how she became a percussionist," signs Mr. Samuels.

"I became seriously ill at the age of seven," signs Ms. Elwyn. "And when I recovered, I found out that I had lost my hearing. I was deaf." "What did you do then?" signs Moses.

[MY] FRIENDS   AND   I   ARE DEAF

I   WORKED HARD.

MY   HEART   WAS SET ON

BECOMING

A PERCUSSIONIST

AND

I

DID.

"Now you can play on my musical instruments," Ms. Elwyn signs. "Come with me, children."

Anna plays on the marimba . . .
Beverly strikes the triangle . . .

Mark pounds the floor tom and the cymbal . . .
Dianne beats the tom-toms . . .
John hits the snare drum . . .
and Moses thumps the bass drum . . .

David strikes the gong . . .
Tommy and Suzy play on the tubular bells . . .

while Steve bangs the kettledrum and Maria plays the congas.

"Children! We have to go!" Mr. Samuels announces after a while.
"Ms. Elwyn has to get ready for another concert."
Moses and his classmates sign thank you, and they wave goodbye
to Ms. Elwyn.

THANKS GOODBYE

On the bus on the way home, Moses signs, "It was so much fun!"

BUS

SO MUCH

FUN

That night, Moses tells his parents about the concert. Here is what he says:

WHEN　　　　　　YOU

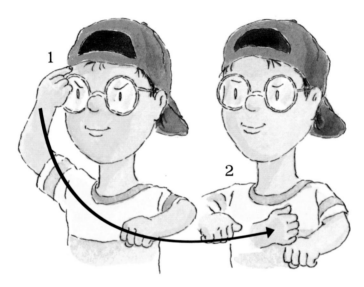

SET YOUR MIND TO IT,　　　　　YOU

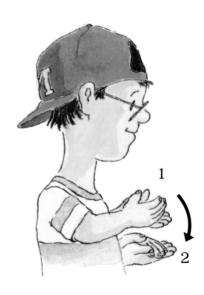

CAN　　　　　BECOME

ANYTHING

YOU

WANT

WHEN

YOU

GROW UP...

A DOCTOR,

ARTIST,

TEACHER,

LAWYER,

FARMER,

ELECTRICIAN,

OR

ACTOR.

I

WANT

TO BECOME

A PERCUSSIONIST.

HAND ALPHABET